WHERE DID DEER GO?

Written by
Joseph Tenney

Illustrated by
Zaki Al-Muhtaseb

I just shot my first deer, what should I do now?

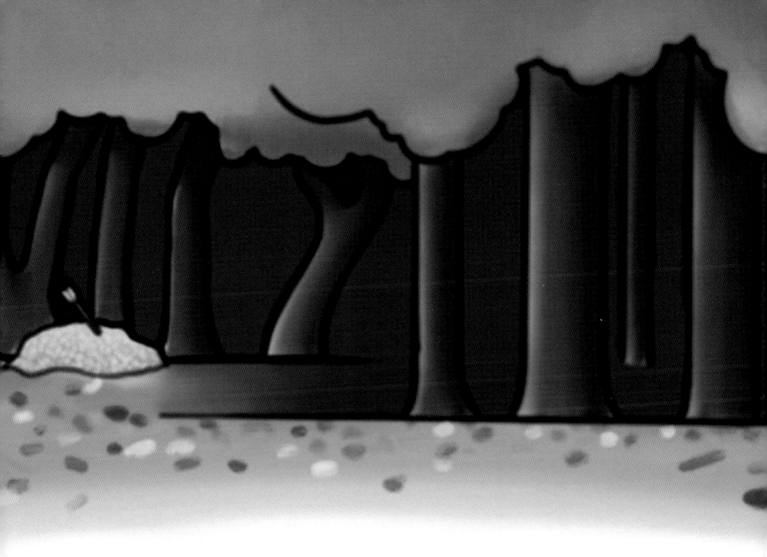

I'm going to get my little tracking dog to help.

My little tracking dog and I go look on the ground. I found my arrow it's all red but...

Where did my deer go?

My little tracking dog smells the ground. She can smell the deer. I see red on the ground but ...

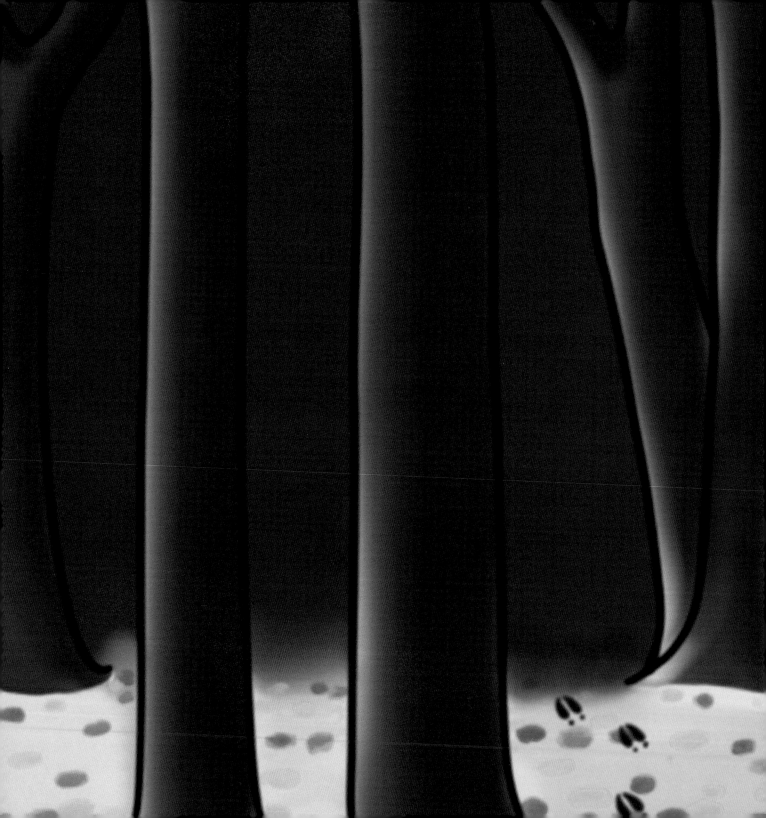

Where did my deer go?

My little tracking dog follows the smell with her nose. She pulls me into the woods with her nose on the ground but...

Where did my
deer go?

My little tracking dog stops in the tall grass. Some of the grass is flat and laying down. We found some red and some hair on the tall grass but...

Where did my deer go?

My little tracking dog starts smelling each path and wants to go down one. I follow her.

My little tracking dog walks through the tall grass and into the woods. Her nose is on the ground. We come to thick briars.

My little tracking dog walks into the briars. I follow her. I see my dogs tail wagging.

She found my deer.
I give my tracking
dog lots of hugs and
kisses, she saved
the day.

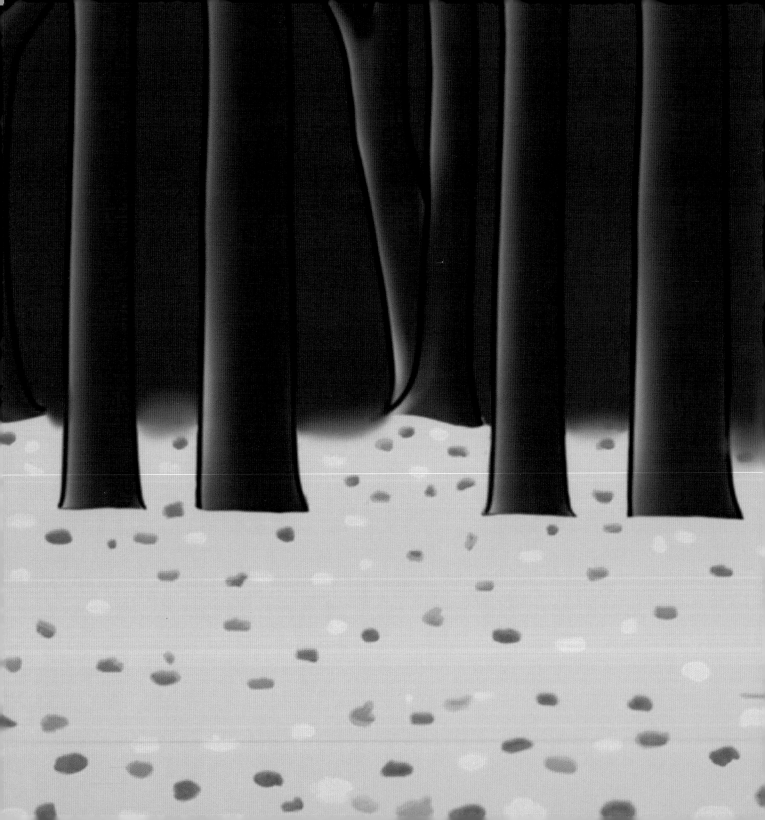